ADAPTED BY KATE HOWARD

SCHOLASTIC INC.

ISBN 978-0-545-66384-7

10 9 8 7 6 5 4 3 2 1 14 15 16 17 18 19/0

Printed in the U.S.A. 40
First printing, July 2014

NINJA ON THE RUN

In New Ninjago City, evil forces were at work. “Tell me where the Golden Ninja is!” the Overlord screamed at Sensei Wu.

Nindroids had been searching for all five ninja for days. But they hadn’t found them—or the Techno-Blades.

“I’ll never tell you,” Sensei Wu vowed.

“You might not . . . but your memories will!” the Overlord cackled.

“This is a perfect place to lay low,” Lloyd told Cole, Jay, Kai, Zane, and Nya. He looked around the monastery. “No robots, no cameras—no problems.”

“Lloyd?” a voice said. It was Misako, Lloyd’s mom. “What are you doing here?”

Lloyd gave her a hug. “The Overlord’s back, and New Ninjago City has fallen under his control. He has Sensei Wu.”

“Where is Lord Garmadon?” Kai asked.

“Here, he is Sensei Garmadon,” Misako said. “Come in . . . but no weapons. Garmadon has sworn an oath never to fight again.”

“But we’re supposed to protect the Techno-Blades with our lives,” Kai said.

“You guys go ahead,” Zane offered. “I’ll watch over them.”

FIGHT WITHOUT FIGHTING

Inside, the ninja found Sensei Garmadon. "Son, so glad you could join us," he said. "Tonight's lesson is the Art of the Silent Fist—to fight without fighting."

Garmadon asked Lloyd to demonstrate.

As the other ninja practiced, Zane jumped up. The Techno-Blades were missing!

There was a rustling sound in the trees. He was not alone!

Zane raced through the orchard. Finally, he came face-to-face with . . . "Pixal! What are you doing here?"

"Discontinuing an old droid," the Overlord's assistant said, attacking him.

Kai heard Pixal and Zane fighting. "The Techno-Blades!"

The other four ninja followed him outside.

"How did she find us?" Cole asked.

"She was only doing what she was programmed to do," Zane said. He touched his Techno-Blade to her forehead, and Pixal's eyes turned green.

“How did you find us?” Zane asked.

“They’ve mined Sensei Wu’s memory,” Pixal said. “The Overlord wants the Golden Ninja and his power!”

“What makes the Techno-Blades so important?” Kai asked.

“They can reboot the system and destroy the Overlord for good,” Pixal explained.

Suddenly, Pixal remembered something. “I didn’t come alone!”

“Who else is with you?” Jay asked.

“Nindroids,” Pixal said.

“NINDROIDS?!” the ninja cried.

They were surrounded!

SNEAK ATTACK!

The Nindroids pounced. Though there were more of them, the ninja were smarter fighters.

Sensei Garmadon joined the battle. He fought without fighting—and it worked. The Nindroids began to crash into one another!

Lloyd powered up his golden energy, but Nya stopped him. "No! Your power only strengthens them!"

“Let’s get out of here!” Nya shouted.

“Anyone want to clear a path?” Jay asked.

“I’ve got an idea,” Cole said. He led them to a waterwheel, and the ninja hopped on. The waterwheel rolled down the hill, scattering all the Nindroids in its path. It was the perfect escape!

“If the Overlord wants my son, I’m not letting him out of my sight,” Garmadon said.

Lloyd nodded. “But if he wants me, and the Techno-Blades are the only thing that can stop him, shouldn’t we split up?”

Nya nodded. “You two go find shelter in my Samurai X cave. The rest of us will shut down the power in New Ninjago City.”

Back in New Ninjago City, the Overlord was furious. “What do you mean they’re not there?!” the Overlord screamed.

“We’ve been tricked,” General Cryptor said.

“Your Nindroids have failed, General Cryptor . . . but my next creation won’t!” the Overlord growled.

STEALTH MISSION

The ninja found a sneaky way to get past the Nindroids guarding New Ninjago City. They hid inside a circus caravan!

"We owe you one," Kai said, hopping out of a magician's box. "Thanks."

The magician waved his magic wand. "We can get you to the Storm Farms, but you're on your own with the Power Substation."

"So, Nya," Cole said, "can we really destroy the Overlord and his Nindroids by simply flipping a switch?"

"Cripple them, yes . . . destroy, no," Nya answered. "Once we've powered down his army, we still need to reboot the central computer with the Techno-Blades."

While the others planned their attack, Pixal helped put Zane back together. He'd been hurt badly during the Nindroid battle.

"Thank you for repairing me," Zane said, smiling. "I guess an old Nindroid like me is no match against the newer models."

THE SAMURAI X CAVE

Out in the desert, Lloyd and Sensei Garmadon followed Zane's falcon. "The Samurai X symbol!" Lloyd gasped.

Lloyd pressed the symbol, and the creature's giant skull yawned open. There was a secret passage!

Inside were dozens of weapons and vehicles. Garmadon spotted a Samurai Raider—a perfect getaway vehicle!

Lloyd tried to hop into the driver's seat, but his dad blocked him. "I swore off fighting . . . not driving."

"Where to now?" Lloyd yelled as they zoomed away.

"As far away as possible!" Garmadon said.

POWER DOWN

Meanwhile, the ninja had reached the Overlord's power station. Nindroid guards surrounded it.

"This is where all of Ninjago gets its power," Zane told Pixal.

"If we want to get in, we have to stay out of sight. We can't take them all on," Nya said.

"I'll stay back," Pixal offered. She would keep watch.

As the ninja sneaked toward the power station, General Cryptor warned his Nindroids, "Keep your eyes out for ninja."

Then Cryptor stopped and laughed at one of his droids—it was tiny. "Look at you! Ran out of metal, did they? I will call you Min-droid. Ha-ha!"

Meanwhile, the ninja had found their way to the station's control room. In the center, something was glowing behind glass.

"That's the power core," Nya said. "Shut that down and it's lights out for the Overlord. If only we knew which switch . . ."

They pushed buttons, but nothing happened.

"There has to be an easier way!" Cole said.

While the ninja were hunting around inside the control room, the Nindroids were lining up outside the door. They were ready to attack!

"Knock-knock . . ." General Cryptor said quietly.

Suddenly, an alarm rang out. Pixal had seen the Nindroids!

"Nindroids!" Nya shouted. "Our cover is blown!"

"Pixal!" Zane ran out of the control room. As he opened the door, the tiny Min-droid rolled in.

"Great, now they come in fun-size!" Jay groaned.

Garmadon and Lloyd were also under attack. The Overlord had created a powerful new machine—a giant MechDragon! It was racing toward Garmadon and Lloyd.

"He's gaining on us!" Lloyd yelled.

Back at the power station, General Cryptor had taken Pixal prisoner.

Zane fought his way through an army of Nindroids. *"Ninjaaaa-GO!"* He took his Techno-Blade and spun through the air.

"You're the original Nindroid," General Cryptor laughed. "Nothing more than a tin can with feelings."

Nya and the ninja were still trying to shut down the control center. But Min-droid kept attacking them.

"Hack him with the Techno-Blade!" Kai shouted to Cole.

Cole swung his weapon—and missed. "I'm trying! I gotta hand it to this little runt. He doesn't know when to quit."

LIGHTS OUT

The Min-droid fired a laser at them. Cole ducked. The blast hit the power core, cracking the glass around it.

"That's it!" Kai said. "Fight without fighting!" He waved at the Min-droid. "Hey, half-pint! Over here!"

The Min-droid fired another laser. Kai ducked—and the glass cracked more.

"We need more Nindroids!" Cole shouted.

Nya opened the door to the control room. The Nindroids swarmed in and began to shoot at the ninja.

The ninja dodged the laser fire. With each shot, the glass around the power core splintered more and more.

"It's working!" Nya cried.

Elsewhere in Ninjago, Lloyd and Sensei Garmadon were still trying to escape the Overlord's MechDragon. The dragon was getting closer and closer. . . .

Back at the power station, Min-droid lunged at the ninja. They ducked out of his way, and—

He smashed into the power core! POW!

In an instant, the robotic dragon crashed to the ground. All the Overlord's other creations shut down. New Ninjago City went dark.

"We did it!" Kai shouted. They had defeated the Nindroids—and the Overlord!

Out in Ninjago, Lloyd and his father knew their friends had succeeded—for now, at least.

"Is it safe to go back?" Lloyd asked.

Garmadon shook his head. "They may have turned off the power, but they still need to reboot the system. Until we know the Overlord is gone for good, we must keep moving."